A

MASQUE

OF

MR PUNCH

A
MASQUE
OF
MR PUNCH

by

ROBERTSON
DAVIES

Toronto
OXFORD UNIVERSITY PRESS
1963

*Requests for permission
to produce this play
should be directed to*
OXFORD UNIVERSITY PRESS
*70 Wynford Drive,
Don Mills (Toronto), Ont.*

Printed in Canada by
T. H. BEST PRINTING COMPANY LIMITED

FOR

THE

BOYS

OF

U.C.C. PREP.

Characters

EVENING-PAPER CRITIC
MORNING-PAPER CRITIC
TELEVISION MAN
TELEVISION WOMAN
PUBLIC-RELATIONS MAN
PUNCH
JUDY
PRETTY POLLY
HARLEQUIN
TOBY THE DOG
DOCTOR
OFFICER
JACK KETCH
DEVIL
LADY IN EVENING DRESS
ADJUDICATOR
AMERICAN PLAYWRIGHT
EUROPEAN PLAYWRIGHT
PROFESSOR
KING PUNCH
PRETTY PAULINA
QUEEN JUDY
GHOST OF PRINCE OMLET
SECOND DEVIL
MEPHISTOPHELES
SCHOOLBOYS
LADIES & GENTLEMEN
ATTENDANTS
USHER

FIRST PERFORMANCE

UPPER CANADA COLLEGE, TORONTO

29 November 1962

Evening-Paper Critic	J. S. BORLAND
Morning-Paper Critic	M. A. ORR
Television Man	M. A. ARONSON
Television Woman	F. T. ROONEY
Public-Relations Man	P. D. MELTZER
Punch	J. D. DEEKS
Judy	A. G. SELLERS
Pretty Polly	P. G. CHADSEY
Harlequin	J. A. PATTILLO
Toby the Dog	A. R. BORNET
Doctor	D. R. GIBSON
Officer	P. G. CREAN
Jack Ketch	J. T. PEPALL
Devil	D. P. TEMPLE
Lady in Evening Dress	H. C. G. UNDERWOOD
Adjudicator	M. H. WEBB
American Playwright	P. A. WHITMORE
European Playwright	D. J. HERINGTON
Professor	J. L. LEAHY
King Punch	E. J. K. WELLS
Pretty Paulina	C. A. HULTON
Queen Judy	F. M. J. LEVENSTON
Shakespearean Harlequin	W. M. HATCH
Ghost of Prince Omlet	J. T. D. KEYES
Second Devil	G. E. M. MUNRO
Mephistopheles	J. A. PATTILLO

Others

C. M. Alvaer, J. S. D. Arthurs, N. S. Axton, R. R. Baker, J. R. Bateman,
D. B. Brown, J. P. Brown, W. G. Coombs, A. S. Cullen, P. A. H. Daly,
J. C. R. Davies, J. A. A. Deacon, H. T. M. Devlin, G. D. R. Finlay,

D. C. Gilday, D. M. Gilmore, T. A. Godfrey, J. H. Hayley, J. A. Heintz-
man, D. O. Jarvis, P. S. Jenkins, T. C. Jewell, M. J. Johnston, R. W. Jones,
J. W. Kerr, R. D. Lace, R. A. Millar, G. S. Miller, K. J. Morgan, P. D.
Phelan, J. D. Rapp, J. D. Reid, G. K. Roberts, P. R. Simard, G. Thomson,
J. J. Thomson, P. S. Watson, M. S. Yamada.

Director: MICHAEL CARVER

Costumes: UBRIACO   *Scenery:* VERNON MOULD

Music: HENRY ATACK

Introduction

It is the fashion for critics to take careful account of the influences they can detect in a writer's work. Mr Punch has been an influence on me since first, as a small boy, I saw the play that bears his name. Though I have never aspired to be like him (for my knowledge of my limitations is one of my chief defects as an artist), I have often wondered what he would do in some situations that have confronted me. I have admired and coveted his gaiety, his masterful way with physical and metaphysical enemies, and his freedom from remorse. As a literary influence Mr Punch is neither classic nor dramatic, but demonic, without a parallel in life or art.

Never underestimate the influence of a puppet-show. The child Goethe fell under the spell of a box of puppets, and the outcome was the mighty *Faust* which has enriched the world theatre and delighted philosophers ever since. It is a coincidence of little importance (save, perhaps, to astrologers) that I was born on the same day as Goethe, 164 years later; and, although my literary development is as nothing in comparison with his, it is of some interest that I, too, have been haunted all my life by Punch, and have at last written this masque about him for the boys of the Preparatory School of Upper Canada College. Who is to say that one of those boys, nearer to Goethe than I, may not in time write a great philosophic drama about Punch, having first heard of that hero from me? Then I should be an 'influence', which is an honourable—indeed, an enviable—literary achievement.

24 April 1963   ROBERTSON DAVIES
                                       U.C.C. 1928-1932

The curtain rises

on a large hotel drawing-room of mid-Victorian design,
decorated in the dark reds, browns, and greens of the
period. The lighting is at three-quarter power.

   Discovered are the EVENING-PAPER CRITIC, *a well-dressed
newspaperman; the* MORNING-PAPER CRITIC, *a newspaperman of scholarly and refined appearance; the* TELEVISION
MAN, *dressed in a 'beat'* CBC *manner, with an untidy beard;
and the* TELEVISION WOMAN, *with long dirty hair and thick-
rimmed spectacles. All are somewhat caricatured.*

   *They step to the front of the stage and speak in the
portentous, over-phrased manner of a verse chorus in a
play by T. S. Eliot.*

CHORUS

Why, why do we find ourselves assembled here
In this ancient and frankly hideous Victorian hotel room,
We, the flower of Canadian journalism?

SEMI-CHORUS OF TELEVISION MAN & WOMAN

(In which, of course, are included the modern mass media
Of radio, of film, and of course, above all, television;
Noble are these, and dear to the folk of our country.)

I

CHORUS

Not ours to inquire, but to go where our duty calls us;
Not ours to dispute, but to function as public recorders;
Not ours to act, but to suffer the actions of others.
Thus we await what the present occasion may bring us:
Our minds not wholly idle—thinking, and partly
    thinking—
Assured that *Time* will explain, and *Life* illustrate in full
    colour,
All that man knows about earth, or needs to know of the
    heavens.

EVENING-PAPER CRITIC

Well, now we've got that off our chests, should we tell
them plainly what we're up to?

TELEVISION WOMAN

Leave it to me. [*To the audience:*] Ladies and gentlemen,
we've come to interview a distinguished visitor to
Canada—

TELEVISION MAN

That we don't know—

MORNING-PAPER CRITIC

Of whose identity we are as yet unaware. That kind of
sloppy phrasing may be all right for you electronics men,
but we gentlemen of the press insist on something a little
more formal.

TELEVISION MAN & WOMAN

Squares!

EVENING-PAPER CRITIC

Order, please. There must be someone—

TELEVISION MAN
To put us in the picture—

EVENING-PAPER CRITIC
To tell us what we're here for.

MORNING-PAPER CRITIC
Isn't there a public-relations man somewhere?

PUBLIC-RELATIONS MAN
[*Entering briskly, beautifully dressed and self-assured*] Yes,
gentlemen—and ladies. I'm the public-relations man.

ALL
Oh, you are, are you? Well, then, where's the booze?

PUBLIC-RELATIONS MAN
I'm terribly sorry, but our guest insists on serving it himself. And I hardly know how to tell you this, but—

ALL
Yes?

PUBLIC-RELATIONS MAN
It may not be quite what you're used to. No hard liquor.
He spoke about serving port and sherry.

MORNING-PAPER CRITIC
Ah, excellent! Obviously a man of cultivation. Good vin-
tages, I trust?

TELEVISION WOMAN
Oh, you morning-paper men! Always wanting to show
that you're a cut above the rest of us.

3

TELEVISION MAN

What's with this port? Who's this Sherry?

TELEVISION WOMAN

Yes, why the funny drinks?

PUBLIC-RELATIONS MAN

Our guest has old-fashioned tastes. I assure you he means to do you honour. But he does not live in quite the same world as we do.

MORNING-PAPER CRITIC

Ah, I get it! You mean these wines are part of the public image he wants to project?

TELEVISION WOMAN

The gracious-living bit?

EVENING-PAPER CRITIC

Is he a wine salesman?

PUBLIC-RELATIONS MAN

No, no; a famous actor!

TELEVISION MAN

An actor? What's his program?

TELEVISION WOMAN

What studio is he with? MGM? Or is he one of those English actors? Or maybe an Italian?

TELEVISION MAN

A woman! I bet it's a woman! One of those terrific Italian film actresses with teeth of pearl, hair like spun gold, neck

4

like a swan, snowy bosom, tawny flanks, figure of a
Venus—

TELEVISION WOMAN

And feet of clay?

PUBLIC-RELATIONS MAN

No, gentlemen; there is no deception. He's a male.

EVENING-PAPER CRITIC

A man?

PUBLIC-RELATIONS MAN

A male. And the fact is . . . he's rather old.

EVENING-PAPER CRITIC

Some flop from the Old World who thinks he can make
good here!

PUBLIC-RELATIONS MAN

No, no! He's famous, beloved. An astounding personality.
Long-standing literary associations, too. And he's always
had his own theatre.

MORNING-PAPER CRITIC

His name! Let's have his name!

PUBLIC-RELATIONS MAN

He has several: Monsieur Polichinelle—

TELEVISION WOMAN

French! We'll use him in Quebec; they don't care how old
actors are down there.

PUBLIC-RELATIONS MAN
Also Signor Punchinello.

TELEVISION WOMAN
Italian! I said so. A great lover?

PUBLIC-RELATIONS MAN
An *unusual* lover.

MORNING-PAPER CRITIC
Not too unusual for a family newspaper, I hope?

PUBLIC-RELATIONS MAN
No, no. His wife is travelling with him—

TELEVISION MAN
She old too?

PUBLIC-RELATIONS MAN
About his own age.

MORNING-PAPER CRITIC
Wonderful! We'll build it up as a great romance! They'll
be the idols of all the Old-Age Pensioners in the country—
and *they're* nearly a majority now, you know.

TELEVISION WOMAN
Sure! We'll show them walking into the sunset of life,
courageously, hand-in-hand, upheld by a great love that has
ripened in the sun like a beautiful tomato—

[*Suddenly from offstage high-pitched voices are heard crying:* 'I will!', 'You won't!', 'I will!', 'You won't!', 'Oh you
6

villain, you monster!', 'Take that, you old bag of bones!', 'Give me the baby!', 'There's your baby!' *The figure of a baby, in a frilled bonnet and a long dress, is flung across the stage and strikes the scenery with a thud. JUDY rushes onstage and seizes it.*]

JUDY

Oh, what a precious! Come to your mammy! There, there, pretty Baby! Was it a pretty diddums, then? And was its pa a horrible monster? There, there, pretty Baby! [*JUDY is a grotesque figure in an Early Victorian gown and bonnet, with a huge nose and chin, like PUNCH himself who now enters (as the lights come up to full power), singing to the tune of 'Marbrouk':*]

PUNCH
Mr Punch is a jolly good fellow,
His coat is all scarlet and yellow.

Hello, everybody! Didn't know you'd come! Glad to see you! Glad to see you!

JUDY
Punch, you villain, you'll kill our precious hinfink!

PUNCH
Rubbish, I won't!

JUDY
You will! And you'll hang for it, just you see if you don't!

PUNCH
Hold your jaw, you old scarecrow. All it wants is artificial resuspiration. Give me a hold of it. [*He seizes Baby and,*

7

*holding it by its feet, swings it rapidly round in a circle.
Baby yells.*] There. Good as new. You don't understand the
care and feeding of children, you don't. I do. Taught
Dr Spock everything he knows. [*Turning toward the
wings, he shouts:*] Polly! Pretty Polly!

[PRETTY POLLY, *dressed as a Victorian nurse-maid but wearing short skirts like a ballet girl, runs in.*]

PUNCH
[*Handing Baby to* POLLY] Here, my darling. Take young
Nuisance for a walk in the park.

POLLY
Oh, law, Mr Punch, you've dirtied Baby's clothes with
your rough ways.

PUNCH
Do what I tell you or I'll cut your head off. And I wouldn't
want to spoil your looks, my delicious dumpling. [*To the
REPORTERS as POLLY runs off:*] A dear girl; a sweet girl; but
doesn't know how to mind what she's told.

PUBLIC-RELATIONS MAN
Mr Punch, if I might have your attention for just a
moment—

PUNCH
Oh, you have it; you have it.

PUBLIC-RELATIONS MAN
May I introduce the ladies and gentlemen of the press?
8

PUNCH
[*Shaking hands all round*] Charmed! Delighted! Enraptured! Busting with joy to see you!

PUBLIC-RELATIONS MAN
And la Signora Punchinello.

PUNCH
My old woman. Do your devours, Judy.

JUDY
[*Curtsying very rapidly to each REPORTER*] How-de-do! Ain't it fine for the time of year! How-de-do! Where did you get that hat? How-de-do! Will you take a drop to drink—

REPORTERS
Drink!

PUNCH
Oho, you're dry, are you? Well, what d'ye think of this? [*He claps his hands and HARLEQUIN pushes on a Victorian bar. JUDY runs behind it and serves the REPORTERS with splendid drinks in attractive colours.*]

PUBLIC-RELATIONS MAN
Have you everything you want, gentlemen? Everybody happy? Good! Now, I thought that this might be an opportunity for a little press conference, so that Monsieur Polichinelle could explain what he has in mind.

[*All REPORTERS produce their notebooks.*]

EVENING-PAPER CRITIC
Good. Mr Punch, what brings you to Canada?

PUNCH
Oh, thought I might do a little work here.

MORNING-PAPER CRITIC
Acting, you mean?

PUNCH
What else?

TELEVISION MAN
That isn't going to be easy. Got your union card?

PUNCH
My talent is my union card.

[*The REPORTERS laugh uproariously.*]

TELEVISION WOMAN
You know, he might go over at that. A few cracks like that one and he could be a sort of small-time Mort Sahl—

TELEVISION MAN
No. Wrong personality. Look, Mr Punch, you might as well know it first as last: you're not what we'd call contemporary, you know.

PUNCH
Meaning what?

TELEVISION WOMAN
You're out of date.

PUNCH

But I haven't been out of work for three hundred years—
a little longer, as a matter of fact. Don't you think I know
my job?

EVENING-PAPER CRITIC

We don't want to hurt your feelings, but three hundred
years is quite an age for an actor. How's your memory?

PUNCH

My memory?

TELEVISION MAN

Yes. Ever have any trouble remembering your lines?

PUNCH

I don't remember 'em. I make 'em up.

TELEVISION WOMAN

Oh? That could be good, you know. That's really contemporary. Gets rid of the author, which is always an impor-
tant beginning to any serious work in the theatre.

TELEVISION MAN

But what would you act? I mean, have you got anything
you could offer to a sponsor, for instance?

PUNCH

Well, I've brought my play.

TELEVISION MAN

And your company? That's different.

PUNCH

But of course. Look, you people don't seem to understand who I am. I've been a popular figure for a very long time.

MORNING-PAPER CRITIC

What my electronic colleagues want to say, Mr Punch, is that we've become rather skeptical of actors from abroad. We have to be shown.

PUNCH

Want to see my show? That's easy. Get me an audience and we'll do it for you.

EVENING-PAPER CRITIC

What, right now?

PUNCH

Why not? But I must have an audience.

MORNING-PAPER CRITIC

Aren't we audience enough?

PUNCH

Do you take me for a fool? Do a show for nothing but critics! It'd be the death of me. No, get me some people— real people. [HARLEQUIN *produces a drum and a trumpet.* PUNCH *seizes the* MORNING-PAPER CRITIC.] Here, you take the drum and beat it. [*He snatches the* TELEVISION WOMAN.] And you blow the trumpet. Come on, get me an audience.

[TELEVISION WOMAN *cannot make the trumpet blow.* MORNING-PAPER CRITIC *taps the drum in a very gentlemanly manner and looks about, half-ashamed, as he says:*]

12

MORNING-PAPER CRITIC
Ah . . . would anyone be interested in a little play? I don't suppose anybody wants to see a play, do they? I mean, I guarantee nothing, but—

PUNCH
You don't expect to get paying customers *that* way, do you?

TELEVISION WOMAN
Actually, we're used to a captive audience, you know. Captive or none at all—that's our way.

MORNING-PAPER CRITIC
I feel a perfect fool. I don't know how to get people into theatres—it's my job to keep them out, if I can. Your whole notion of theatre is vulgar—

PUNCH
'Course it's vulgar. And *I'm* vulgar! Gimme that there drum! I'll show you how to bring 'em in! [*He beats the drum with professional fury, and* JUDY *blows the trumpet. At once a crowd of* SCHOOLBOYS *begins to appear. They are wearing blazers, and they sit on steps leading down from the stage.*]

PUNCH'S SONG
Walk up, walk up for Punch's Show!
Walk up for Punchinello!
Worth twice the money; in you go
And see the comical fellow.

He'll make you laugh,
He'll make you cry,

He'll make you scream and yell—O!
　　Mr Punch
　　And Mr Joe,
　　Mr Nell
　　And Mr Lo—
　　Mr Punchinello!

PUNCH, JUDY, & HARLEQUIN
Mrs Judy, Toby too,
　　Winsome Pretty Polly;
Gallant soldier, all in blue,
　　Harlequin so jolly.

He'll make you laugh,
He'll make you cry,
He'll make you scream and yell—O!
　　Mr Punch
　　And Mr Joe,
　　Mr Nell
　　And Mr Lo—
　　Mr Punchinello!

SCHOOLBOYS
Come on, come on, we mustn't be late,
　　Drum and trumpet sounding;
Put a penny on Toby's plate,
　　Set your feet a-pounding.

He'll make you laugh,
He'll make you cry,
He'll make you scream and yell—O!
　　Mr Punch

And Mr Joe,
Mr Nell
And Mr Lo—
Mr Punchinello!

[*When* PUNCH *begins to sing, small groups of* LADIES &
GENTLEMEN *come in. As they listen to the song, they laugh
and become excited.* TOBY *runs in with his cup in his
mouth, and all the* SPECTATORS *drop pennies into it.* JUDY
*also collects money, and she gives an occasional squall on
the trumpet. The character of the entertainment changes
greatly.* PRETTY POLLY *runs onstage and helps* HARLEQUIN
*to set up a small but pretty backdrop: both then disappear
behind it with* TOBY. *The backdrop represents an old-
fashioned street drawn in the sharp perspective of the
seventeenth century, and it is against this that the action
of Punch's play is performed.*]

PUNCH [*Bowing*]
Ladies and gentlemen, pray how do you do?
If you are all happy, I'm happy too.
Stop and hear my merry little play;
If I don't make you laugh, I'll give back your pay.

TELEVISION WOMAN
What's that?

PUNCH
That's my prologue.

TELEVISION WOMAN
Oh, but *you* can't speak the prologue. The leading actor
mustn't appear till later on. But don't worry, we'll rewrite
it for you according to modern ideas.

15

PUNCH

Dear, sweet, beautiful child, I have been acting this play for about three hundred years. So hold your gab!

SPECTATORS

Sh! Let Punch go on! Quiet!

[*PUNCH bows. Enter the dog TOBY.*]

PUNCH

Hello, Toby! Who called you? I hope you're very well, Mr Toby.

TOBY

Bow-wow-wow!

PUNCH

How's your master, Harlequin? How's my good friend Harlequin?

TOBY

Bow-wow-wow!

PUNCH

I'm glad to hear it. Good dog! That's a fine fellow! No wonder his master is so fond of him. Would you like a biscuit, Toby?

TOBY

Bow-wow-wow!

PUNCH

Here's a lovely biscuit for you. Now, roll over sir! [*TOBY does so.*] Now, die for your country. [*TOBY shams dead.*]

16

Now beg. [*TOBY begs. PUNCH puts the biscuit on TOBY's nose.*] Trust! [*TOBY is motionless.*] Good dog. Good Toby. [*TOBY snaps up the biscuit.*] Now for a little joke. [*He takes a sandwich from the table and sprinkles pepper in it, confiding to the audience:*] Cayenne: wonderful worm-conditioner! [*TOBY begs again and PUNCH puts the sandwich on TOBY's nose. TOBY gobbles it and has a fit while PUNCH roars with laughter.*]

TOBY
[*Growling*] Ruff! Rrruff-ruff-ruff!

PUNCH
Now, now, Toby. What's the matter? Did you get out of bed the wrong way this morning? Here, boy! [*He holds out a hoop covered with paper. After some coaxing, TOBY jumps through it. The SPECTATORS applaud.*] Good Toby! Thank you, ladies and gentlemen. All done with kindness, as you see! Good Toby! [*He leans down to pat TOBY, who seizes PUNCH's nose and drags him around the stage.*] Oh Judy, Judy my dear! My nose! My pretty little nose! Harlequin! Come here and see what your nasty dog has done!

[*Enter HARLEQUIN with a skip and a jump, carrying a slapstick in his hand. He hits PUNCH and TOBY with a great noise. TOBY lets PUNCH go.*]

HARLEQUIN
Here, you, Mr Punch! What are you doing to my poor dog?

PUNCH
Oh, Harlequin. Glad to see you looking so well.

HARLEQUIN

Have you been beating and ill-using my dog, Mr Punch?

PUNCH

He has been biting and ill-using my poor nose. What have you got there, sir?

HARLEQUIN

A fiddle.

PUNCH

Oh. And do you play on your fiddle?

HARLEQUIN

Come here and you'll see. What shall I play?

PUNCH

Oh, play the Refrain from Spitting. [*HARLEQUIN pretends to play the stick while a fiddle plays in the orchestra.*] Oh, exquisite! Oh, ravishing! Can you teach me to play like that?

HARLEQUIN

Indeed I can. Just come closer, Mr Punch. [*He beats PUNCH with the slapstick while TOBY barks and snaps at PUNCH. PUNCH runs offstage right. While HARLEQUIN is bowing to the SPECTATORS, PUNCH rushes in from the left with a huge club and aims a terrible blow at HARLEQUIN, who sees PUNCH and runs away.*]

PUNCH

You villain! Come back and fight like a man! [*Coaxing*] Come back, Harlequin, and let me play to you on *my* fiddle. [*HARLEQUIN rushes in, thumbs his nose at* PUNCH, *and dashes away.*] The sneak, he suspects me. Judy!

JUDY

[*Offstage*] What is it, my own Punchy-wunchy?

PUNCH

There's a wife for you! What a precious darling creature. Come here, my love!

JUDY

[*Entering with Baby in her arms*] What do you want, I say?

PUNCH

A kiss! A pretty kiss! [*He kisses* JUDY, *who slaps him.*]

JUDY

Take that! How do you like my kisses? Will you have another?

PUNCH

Judy, my love, I've had a disagreement with our neighbour Harlequin, and he set his horrid dog on me. Run after him, my love, and call him back here so I can play to him on my fiddle.

JUDY

Hold Baby, Punch. I'll send Polly to take care of it. [*She goes.*]

PUNCH

What a precious wife! Worth a thousand a year! There, Baby, don't you cry. [*He sings to Baby:*]

19

> *Rock-a-bye baby,*
> *On the tree top—*

Oh, do stop your noise, you little horror!

> *When the wind blows,*
> *The cradle will rock.*

Was there ever such a baby for crying! Hold your gab, you little wretch!

> *When the bough breaks—*

That's enough. Daddy will be very, very cross. [*He shakes Baby and, when it does not stop howling, twirls it rapidly a few times and tosses it up into the sky where it disappears.*] And don't come back till you're in a better temper.

[*Enter* POLLY.]

PUNCH

Oh, there you are, you pretty creature! [*He sings from* The Beggar's Opera:]

> *When the heart of a man is depressed with care,*
> *All the mists are dispelled when a woman appears—*

POLLY

Where's Baby, Mr Punch?

PUNCH

Gone to see a man about a dog.

POLLY

What—Baby?

PUNCH

Oh, no, that was Judy. Baby's gone—on a space-flight. Baby's a space-ape now. It'll be back. Do you love me, Polly?

POLLY

Oh, sir! What would Missus say?

PUNCH

Do you think I'm a handsome man, Polly? A fine figure of a man?

[*Baby's bonnet floats down to the stage.*]

POLLY

Mr Punch, have you done something dreadful to Baby?

PUNCH

Only for your sake, my charmer. So that you could be alone—with me.

POLLY

Oh, you cruel wretch, you've killed dear Baby. Oh, you barbarian!

PUNCH

Don't cry so, my dear. You'll cry your pretty eyes out, and that would be a pity.

POLLY

Oh, how could you kill poor Baby?

PUNCH

Jealousy. Who got all your kisses? Poor Baby! Who had all your pats and caresses? That dratted Baby! Jealousy raged in my buzzem like a three-alarm fire! He came between us, so I killed him. But if you cry, I must cry too. Look, I'm crying!

POLLY

[*Aside*] What a handsome young man Mr Punch is! It's a pity he should cry so. See how the tears run down his beautiful long nose. [*To* PUNCH:] If you killed Baby for love of me, I really must forgive you.

PUNCH

I could kill *myself* for love of you, let alone a nasty baby! [*He plays his stick across his arm, like a violin bow, and sings with immense feeling:*]

> *When I think on you, my jewel,*
> *   Wonder not my heart is sad;*
> *You're so fair and yet so cruel,*
> *   You're enough to drive me mad.*

[*As* POLLY *moves about the stage,* PUNCH *follows her on his knees.*]

> *On thy lover show thy pity:*
> *   And relieve his bitter smart.*
> *Think you Heaven has made you pretty,*
> *   But to break your lover's heart?*

POLLY

Oh, Mr Punch, I don't know what to say! Do you truly love me?

22

PUNCH

I do, I do. [*He sings, to a polka tune:*]

> *I love you so, I love you so,*
> *I never will leave you, no, no, no;*
> *If I had all the wives of wise King Sol,*
> *I would kill them all for my pretty Pretty Poll.*

[*POLLY now joins in the song, and they dance the polka.*]

PUNCH & POLLY

> *Tol-lol-lol, tol-lol-lol,*
> *Handsome Punch and pretty Pretty Poll;*
> *Fondly, fondly Punch will loll*
> *Upon the buzzem of his pretty Pretty Poll.*

[*PUNCH and POLLY continue to dance, repeating the song together. JUDY returns; POLLY runs off in dismay. JUDY sets upon PUNCH and beats him soundly with his own stick.*]

JUDY

Oh, you villain! You deceiver! You'd break the heart of a brazen image, you would! [*Baby's dress floats down from above.*] What have you done with Baby? A-heaving and a-tossing of my precious child, and a-carrying on with that hussy behind my back! Oh, Punch, some day I'll forget myself and do you a mischief, so I will! [*She has beaten him thoroughly, and now rushes off in a temper. PUNCH lies on the floor.*]

PUNCH

Oh, I'm murdered! I'm a dead man! Will nobody save my life? Doctor, doctor! Come and bring me to life again. Doctor! Doctor!

[*Enter the* DOCTOR. *He wears eighteenth-century dress and carries a bag of tools.*]

DOCTOR

Who calls so loud?

PUNCH

Oh, heavens! Oh, mercy! Murder!

DOCTOR

What is the matter? Bless me, who is this? My good friend Mr Punch? Taking a nap on the grass after dinner?

PUNCH

Doctor, I've been killed.

DOCTOR

[*Takes* PUNCH's *pulse, using an hour-glass for a watch.*] No, no, Mr Punch; not so bad as that, sir. I assure you, as a medical man, that you are not killed.

PUNCH

Then I've lost my powers of speech.

DOCTOR

Why, so you have. Where are you hurt? Is it here? [*Touches* PUNCH's *head.*]

PUNCH

No, lower.

DOCTOR

Here, then? [*Touches* PUNCH's *chest.*]

24

No; lower still.

DOCTOR

Then is your handsome leg broken? [*Tries the leg for a knee-jerk.*]

PUNCH

[*Kicking the* DOCTOR *in the eye*] Don't do that, it tickles! [*He jumps up and staggers about the stage, laughing, while the* DOCTOR *produces an enormous syringe from his case and chases him.*] What's that?

DOCTOR

Medicine, Mr Punch, to calm your nerves. [*Jabbing* PUNCH *in a convenient spot, he presses home the plunger.*]

PUNCH

Is that what they call a tranquillizer?

DOCTOR

That's exactly what it is. Come here for another dose.

PUNCH

But Doctor, I'm the peaceablest man that ever lived. You're the angry one. Why don't you have a jab of that yourself?

DOCTOR

Doctors never take medicine. You ought to know that.

PUNCH

Turn about is fair play, Doctor. [*He struggles with the* DOCTOR *and gets the syringe. Baby's vest falls from above.*

The DOCTOR *turns to see what it is and, as he bends over,* PUNCH *shoves the needle sharply into his posterior. The* DOCTOR *reels, then falls dead.*] There, I knew it. Doctors always die when they take their own medicine. Now, Doctor, cure yourself if you can.

[*Enter* JUDY *followed by an* OFFICER.]

JUDY

There's the villain. Seize him! Officer, do your duty!

OFFICER

I arrest you, Mr Punch, in the Queen's name.

PUNCH

Are you by any chance addressing me, my good fellow?

OFFICER

I arrest you, at the suit of this lady.

PUNCH

Go away. Can't talk to common fellows in the street. As for that old woman, she's just trying to scrape acquaintance with me. Curse my fatal beauty!

OFFICER

It won't do, you know, Mr Punch. You've killed your baby.

PUNCH

It was my own baby, wasn't it? If I'd killed somebody else's baby, there might be some excuse for all this fuss. Officer, are you a married man?

OFFICER

That I am, sir.

PUNCH

Any little ones?

OFFICER

Seventeen, sir, and another expected shortly.

PUNCH

Then you understand the tenderness of a father's heart.
Officer—good, kind Officer—would you by any chance
like to sell me a nice fat baby?

OFFICER

You're a-tempting of a poor man, Mr Punch.

PUNCH

Please? Pretty please?

OFFICER

You're a-trifling with a father's feelings. I couldn't think
of it cheap, mind you.

PUNCH

Ah, but you *will* think of it, won't you? Here am I, child-
less, while you are rich—rich in posterity. Have pity on
the poor! What are babies fetching these days?

OFFICER

I'd have to ask my wife. She has her favourites, you know.

PUNCH

That's a wise man. You just run along and ask her now,
and come back with a lovely baby for poor, broken-hearted
Punch.

[*The* OFFICER *salutes elaborately and marches off.*]

JUDY

It won't do, you know, Punch. I see through your wicked tricks. You shan't deceive me with any old second-hand baby.

[*Another of Baby's garments falls from the sky.*]

PUNCH

Bless me, that plagued Baby seems to be moulting. I wish it would come down. If it doesn't hurry up I shall be in a nasty pickle.

[*Enter* JACK KETCH, *the hangman, carrying a gallows over his shoulder.*]

KETCH

When's the hanging to be?

PUNCH

What hanging?

KETCH

I was told there was to be a hanging. A villain killed his baby. A villain name of Punch. Know anything about him?

PUNCH

You mean Mr Punch? The handsome heart-breaker?

KETCH

I mean ugly old Punch. He's to be hanged.

PUNCH

Hanging. A terribly stuffy death, I've always been told.

28

KETCH

True, master; I should know. Jack Ketch is my name, and Jack Ketch my nature. Hangman, man and boy, this five-and-twenty year. And my father before me. And his father before him.

PUNCH

Oh, a family trade.

KETCH

Ah; there's an art to it, you know.

PUNCH

Family secrets, I suppose? And you'd never tell them. I can see you'd never tell. There's a handsomeness in your face, Mr Ketch—a kind of sublimity, in which honour and dignity are mingled—that makes me warm to you at once.

KETCH

You don't say?

PUNCH

You're the handsomest man—bar one, and I shan't name him now because of modesty—that I ever clapped eyes on. You'd never tell the secrets of your noble profession. Oh, no—not you!

KETCH

Not to everybody, I wouldn't. Not to common riffraff. But a gentleman and a scholar now—

PUNCH

Yes, yes?

29

KETCH

That'd be different. Look, this here's what we call the Instrument.

PUNCH

Oh, it's a handsome article!

KETCH

You may well say that. See—stands firm as a rock. And this here—this noose that hangs down—well, in the profession, that's what we call the Tickler.

PUNCH

The Tickler? Well, I never! And what's the Tickler for, Mr Ketch?

KETCH

Ah, that'd be telling!

PUNCH

But you'd tell me, wouldn't you? I see it in your beautiful blue eyes. You're going to tell.

KETCH

No, I ain't. But . . .

PUNCH

But? But? Come on, don't be an old spoilsport!

KETCH

I dassn't, and that's the truth. It's a trade secret. I dassn't.

PUNCH

Could you just show me? Just a hint? Just the teentsiest, weentsiest hint? [*He gives* KETCH *money.*]

KETCH

Oh, there's no resisting a real gentleman like you. Now watch careful. See? I takes the Tickler, see? And I drops it over my head, see? And I just settles it nice and easy, like the comfortablest scarf your old granny ever knit for her loving grandson, see? And then—

PUNCH

And then—*up he goes!* [*So saying, he pulls the rope and hangs KETCH. He then sings:*]

> *Hurrah! Hurrah! I've done the trick!*
> *Jack Ketch is dead—I'm free!*
> *I do not care now if Old Nick*
> *Himself should come for me!*

JUDY

Punch, you monster, you've robbed me of my justice, and you've robbed me of my child—

PUNCH

Stop! Wait! Do you see something falling? Look, it's getting bigger . . . and bigger . . . and bigger. Catch it, Judy! Catch it, butterfingers!

[*Baby falls out of the sky, without its clothes. PUNCH and JUDY run about to field it. JUDY catches it, and she and PUNCH dance and sing:*]

PUNCH'S POLKA
Punch and Judy,
> *We lead a merry life;*
Punch is the husband
> *And Judy is the wife;*

Punch is the master
But Judy is a shrew,
So when we ain't a-quarrelling,
We don't know what to do.

Prettily we go in Punch's Polka
With a hop and a skip and a one-two-three;
Judy loves Punch and Punch loves Judy,
Oh, what an elegant couple are we!

Punch loves the girls
And the girls they all adore him;
See the pretty darlings
Dropping down before him;
Judy looks as sour
As a crab-apple tree,
'Bless 'em!' says Punch,
But 'Drat 'em!' says she.

Prettily we go in Punch's Polka
With a hop and a skip and a one-two-three;
Judy loves Punch and Punch loves Judy,
Oh, what an elegant couple are we!

Judy loves Baby,
Pretty Baby Dumpling;
Punch kisses Nurse
And gives the brat a rumpling;
Judy beats the Nurse
To larn her and to better her:
So our life goes
With kissing and etceterer.

> Prettily we go in Punch's Polka
>   With a hop and a skip and a one-two-three;
> Judy loves Punch and Punch loves Judy,
>   Oh, what a model of the married life are we!

[*At the end of the song, a terrible thunder is heard. There is a burst of flame and a* DEVIL *appears.*]

DEVIL
Punch, Punch, I've come for you at last!

PUNCH
For me? What have I done? Baby's come back. I am innocent.

DEVIL
Innocent? Who killed Jack Ketch?

PUNCH
Tickler did it!

DEVIL
Who killed the Doctor?

PUNCH
He died of taking his own medicine!

DEVIL
Who poisoned Harlequin's dog?

PUNCH
Harlequin's dog?

33

DEVIL

It bit your great ugly nose and now it's dead!

PUNCH

Good, kind Mr Devil, I never did you any harm, but all the good in my power! There, there . . . don't come any nearer! I hope you and all your respectable family are quite well? . . . Very much obliged to you for this visit, but I won't detain you any longer. Good evening. [*He tries to run away.*]

DEVIL

It's no good, Mr Punch. The game's up. Now you come along with me.

PUNCH

You must be a stupid Devil not to know your best friend when you see him! Come on, then! If you must have a fight, let's see who's the best man—Punch or the Devil. [*There is now a tremendous combat. At first the DEVIL seems to have the best of it and chases PUNCH all over the stage, but PUNCH trips the DEVIL and beats him so that at last he hangs head first from the front of the stage. PUNCH puts his foot on the DEVIL.*] Hurrah! Hurrah! The Devil is dead! The Devil is dead!

[*There is great applause from the SPECTATORS. All the characters from Punch's play come onstage. The DOCTOR leaps to his feet. The gentlemen of the company bow and the ladies curtsy. An USHER from the theatre audience presents JUDY with a huge bouquet of vegetables. Then the REPORTERS move to centre stage to join the actors, who obviously expect to be congratulated. But there is an embarrassing silence.*]

34

PUNCH

Why is everybody so quiet? Isn't anyone going to congratulate us? What did you think of the play?

LADY IN EVENING DRESS

[*Stepping forward from among the* SPECTATORS] We can't tell you until we've heard the Adjudicator.

PUNCH

What's an adjudicator?

LADY IN EVENING DRESS

Oh, Mr Punch, you are terribly out of touch with the theatre as we know it in Canada. The Adjudicator is the man who tells us what to think. We've arranged for one of the very best adjudicators from our Dominion Drama Festival to give his opinion of your presentation, and I think he must have finished making his notes because here he comes now.

[*The* ADJUDICATOR *walks solemnly onto the stage from the theatre audience. He wears ill-fitting dress clothes and a dreadful wig, and carries a huge sheaf of notes which he drops from time to time as he speaks. Only the* REPORTERS *applaud him.*]

ADJUDICATOR

Ladies and gentlemen: the play we have seen tonight must be classified, I suppose, as a not very happy excursion into the Theatre of the Absurd—[PUNCH *protests, but is firmly shushed by the* REPORTERS, *who are busily taking notes.*] This movement, as you know, attempts to explore the disunity, the disconnectedness—what I must call, for want of better words, the fragmented character—of modern

35

life. It is rooted in the despair which every intelligent play-goer feels about the future, the past, and the present. We are all agreed, I am sure, that everything is bad and is rapidly getting worse—that there is, in fact, No Hope. [*There is applause from the* REPORTERS.] Against this over-powering and omnipresent Nullity, man opposes his feeble spirit; but we all recognize that man hasn't a chance. Man is done for, and life is a mess. [*More applause, and a few cheers.*] Now, how has this theme been handled in the play we have just seen? The author has begun well: the frag-mented home, the Freudian jealousy of the protagonist toward his offspring, the sadism which lurks behind the façade of bourgeois life—these have been presented with some power. The mockery of established institutions—the incompetent law enforcement and the brutality of capital punishment—there is a strong influence from the drama of Bert Brecht here, undigested though it seems to be. But the dénouement—the death of the Devil—is utterly un-acceptable. Are we, in the latter half of the twentieth century, to be told that the Devil is dead? Most certainly not; we know better. And the author ought to know better. He should be ashamed of himself. When this play is rewritten, as it ought to be, the Devil must have a bigger part. The Devil must be the hero. [*The* DEVIL *cheers loudly, and is knocked back into his chair by* PUNCH.] This intoler-able Happy Ending utterly discredits a play which other-wise rises almost to the level of the mediocre. Let me assure the author that we shall not build an indigenous Canadian theatre on plays with happy endings. We are miserable or we are nothing. Hope is out of fashion. Now, as for the presentation itself, I can deal with it rapidly. The acting was bad; the setting and lighting were bad; the costumes were bad. On this occasion none of the prizes will be presented except the usual handsome present to the Adjudicator. It is one of the glories of our Canadian theatre that nobody has ever heard of a bad adjudicator. Thank you.

LADY IN EVENING DRESS
That's what we've been waiting for—an expert opinion. But what is to be done?

AMERICAN PLAYWRIGHT
[*Advancing from the audience*] It's a simple problem, really. Let me rewrite the play for you along the lines I have made famous and, if I may say so, profitable.

LADY IN EVENING DRESS
Have we met?

AMERICAN PLAYWRIGHT
Oh, excuse me. I should have introduced myself. I am Swanee River, the celebrated playwright of American Southern Decadence.

LADY IN EVENING DRESS
Swanee River! We are honoured.

AMERICAN PLAYWRIGHT
Thank you kindly, ma'am. Now the first thing is to change Punch into a female character—

PUNCH
Female? Me?

AMERICAN PLAYWRIGHT
Yes. I see you as a Southern Belle who is down on her luck—old plantation gone, old family mansion sunk into

37

the swamp, no money—but still beautiful, still a lady. Except of course that you've taken pretty heavily to drink and dope—

PUNCH

Yes, yes. I think I see myself in a part like that. [*He drapes a cloak around himself as a dress and slinks across the stage as the character described.*] Is this anything like it?

AMERICAN PLAYWRIGHT

Excellent! You inspire me! Go on doing that, you lovely, degraded creature!

[*A voice cries 'Stop!', and a wild-eyed man, the* EUROPEAN PLAYWRIGHT, *rushes onstage. His feet are stuck in a couple of buckets, which somewhat impede his gait.*]

EUROPEAN PLAYWRIGHT

You've got it all wrong! If *Punch* is to be rewritten, it must be in the European style.

AMERICAN PLAYWRIGHT

Just who are you, brother?

EUROPEAN PLAYWRIGHT

I am Samuel Bucket, the outrider of the *avant-garde*. I protest against your sentimental approach to this universal theme.

PUNCH

Oh, I'm being fought over by famous playwrights! An actor's dream. Please, Mr Bucket, what have you in mind for me?

38

Punch, I see your drama in terms of the Anti-Play—the Drama of Nothingness. Now: the scene is a back alley. Two garbage cans stand against a wall; it bears the thrilling message POST NO BILLS, but POST and BILLS have been worn away so that only the word NO is clear to the audience. *No* is the dominant symbol of the play.

PUNCH

Whew! Strong stuff, Bucket! Go on.

EUROPEAN PLAYWRIGHT

In one of the garbage cans, with the lid wired down, is . . . *you!*

PUNCH

Lid wired down?

EUROPEAN PLAYWRIGHT

Right down. In the other garbage can is . . . *nobody at all!*

PUNCH

Not a soul?

EUROPEAN PLAYWRIGHT

Nobody and nothing. Just dirty, smelly emptiness. Now, your character is that of a blind deaf-mute. The drama is your struggle to communicate with the other garbage can.

PUNCH

But I can't talk, and there's nobody there!

39

EUROPEAN PLAYWRIGHT

Precisely. That's the joke, you see. It's a comedy. For three-quarters of an hour nothing whatever happens. Then—curtain.

PUNCH

Oh, no, no, no! I like this gentleman's idea much better. Go on: I'm a beautiful degraded Southern beauty . . .

AMERICAN PLAYWRIGHT

You are selling dope from door to door. A group of under-privileged children attack you and steal all your dope. You bewail your fate—

PUNCH

Bewail my fate . . . oh, I like that.

AMERICAN PLAYWRIGHT

Then the children pull you to pieces and eat you.

PUNCH

Eat me?

AMERICAN PLAYWRIGHT

That's what I said.

PUNCH

My public would never stand for it.

AMERICAN PLAYWRIGHT

The public will stand for anything.

PUNCH

Couldn't I eat them?

AMERICAN PLAYWRIGHT

Absolutely no.

PUNCH

Then I won't play! You've got to find something better.

PROFESSOR

[*Stepping forward from among the* SPECTATORS, *wearing cap and gown*] Excuse me! I must say a word—

LADY IN EVENING DRESS

But we are having a serious artistic discussion.

PROFESSOR

I know. And you've got it all wrong—

ADJUDICATOR

Sir, dare you suggest that an adjudicator can be wrong?

PROFESSOR

Please don't misunderstand me—

ADJUDICATOR

When I have my memoirs ghost-written I'll fix *you*, my good man! Who ever heard of an adjudicator being wrong?

PROFESSOR

But you *are* wrong. You and these modern playwrights. You haven't understood what this play is at all—

PUNCH

Hooray!

PROFESSOR

Because it was presented with the emphasis in the wrong place.

41

What?

PROFESSOR

It is essentially a tragedy—a great revelation of the human spirit under stress. I represent the Board of Governors of the Stratford Shakespearean Festival. By scholarly deductions that I won't trouble you with now, we happen to know that the drama we have just seen is a lost play of Shakespeare's. It had suffered dilapidation over the centuries, but it can easily be restored to its original form—

PUNCH

Oh, am I going to act at Stratford? Oh, joy! The ambition of a lifetime fulfilled! Let Christopher Plummer look to his laurels! Oh, please, please can I act in *Rummy-o and Giblets*?

PROFESSOR

We might be able to give you a walk-on part if you will submit yourself utterly, abjectly, and grovellingly to the will of the Director.

PUNCH

Pooh! Shan't play, then. I'm used to running my own show.

PROFESSOR

You have destroyed a great play. Sit down and see it in its true form.

[*During the foregoing, three pillars and a rostrum have been set up to suggest the Stratford stage. Now the orchestra plays the Stratford fanfare and a gun is shot off.*

The actors in what follows adopt a Stratford Shakespearean style of acting. The first to enter is KING PUNCH, *followed by attendants.*]

KING PUNCH

Oh, heavy heart that feeds upon itself,
Chewing with canker'd tooth sour envy's cud!
Unhappy Punch! Though glorious in the eyes
Of common men, who grossly flatter thee
Because thou'rt handsome, god-like, and a king,
Thy days are torture; and when gentle night
Brings to the world her poppy-drowsy boon,
Thy pillow's stuffed with thorns, and thou, poor Punch,
Count'st every hour told by the watchful clock.
What holds the world, Punch, that thou should'st desire?
What treasure tempts the envy of a king?
—But soft, one comes: down thoughts into my soul!
'Tis she, Paulina, guardian of my jewel.

[*Enter* PRETTY PAULINA, *gathering flowers, and* TOBY.]

PAULINA

Lo, here I wander at this morning hour
To pluck the blossom from each several flower;
The violet, the blushing celandine,
Bright antirrhinum, and sweet columbine,
Soft baby's breath wherein the cuckoo nests,
Fierce mustard, sovran for oppressed chests:
All these I bind into a fragrant posy
To gratify our good Queen Judy's nosy.
And see, on padded paw beside me comes
The faithful Toby, noblest of Dumb Chums.

43

KING PUNCH

Sweet child, where is thy charge? The prince, my son?

PAULINA

Reposing in his royal mother's arms,
Snuffling the sweet air of the fragrant morn.
Look where he comes. [*She gestures offstage.*]

KING PUNCH

    But say, Paulina, holds he
The rattle giv'n him at his christening
By Carabosse, his fairy godmother?

PAULINA

He doth; nor ever will from it be parted.
Oh, 'tis the prettiest sight to see him mouth it,
Thrusting the bauble 'twixt his toothless gums,
Only to pull it forth, all wet, and then,
With gurgling joy, to shove it in again.

KING PUNCH

Oh, there's the wormwood withers up my soul!
I lust to have that rattle, and have't I will!

[*Enter* QUEEN JUDY, *carrying Baby.*]

    QUEEN JUDY [*Sings:*]
    Twang the lyre
    And toot the flute,
     Hey, nonny, nonny:
    Pluck the flower
    And chew the root,

44

My baby's bonny!
Honk the hautboy,
Thump the drum,
Prettiest babe in Christendom,
Ninny, ninny nonny!

KING PUNCH

Her sweet notes pierce my soul! Judy my love—

QUEEN JUDY

My honour'd lord?

KING PUNCH

How does our child, Prince Omlet?

QUEEN JUDY

In the frog's vein, my lord. He swells and swells.

KING PUNCH

[*Aside*] Would he might burst! [*To* QUEEN JUDY:] Judy,
sweet queen, thou know'st—

QUEEN JUDY
My lord?

KING PUNCH
That I, above all things,
Desire Prince Omlet's rattle.

QUEEN JUDY

Omlet's rattle, lord?

KING PUNCH

Prince Omlet's rattle.

QUEEN JUDY

Nay, not Omlet's rattle?

KING PUNCH

Yes, Omlet's rattle! Are thine ears so clogg'd
With mother-love thou can'st not hear my words?

QUEEN JUDY

But Omlet's rattle, lord—

KING PUNCH

        Oh, not again!
Rattle I said, and rattle I do mean;
I want the rattle, therefore hold thy prattle,
Or thou and I shall instantly do battle.

PAULINA

Nay, my lord, nay: consider what thou say'st.
Did not the foul witch Carabosse, when she
Our prince the rattle gave, declare as law
That only he might wield it, and whoe'er
Did, with unlineal hand, that rattle gripe
Should perish, howling, and the world should see
The deep damnation of his taking-off?

KING PUNCH

Prate not to me of Carabosse's curses!
Am I not Punch? Shall not the welkin split
If Punch the tyrant have not his desire?

PAULINA

Oh, this is pride! *Hubris* the Greeks it call'd.
It bodes no good: pride goes before a fall.

Give me the rattle!

Nay!

Then die! [*He stabs* QUEEN JUDY.]

Woe's me,
To have seen what I have seen, see what I see!

[*Sings weakly:*]   *Honk the hautboy*
Thump the drum
Prettiest babe—

Ah me! I die. [*She dies.*]

Alack, my lady's dead—

The rattle, come!

My life before thou harm'st of Omlet's head
A single hair—

No hair has he, therefore
Toothless and bald, he goes to join his dam!
[*He stabs Baby and seizes the rattle.*]

PAULINA

Thou reeking, writhing, raucous, wretched runt!
Woe was the day whenever thou was't born!
Woe was the day thou first bestrode the throne!
Woe was the day Queen Judy thee beheld!
Woe was the day when she to thee was't wived!
In body crooked, crookeder in soul,
Thus to perdition, Punch, I thee commend,
Drench'd in wife's, child's blood, woeful be thy end!

KING PUNCH

And whoa to thee, whoa to thy cantering tongue!
This to thy heart. [*He stabs* PAULINA.] There now, the job
   is done.

[*KING PUNCH exits, whirling the rattle happily, and* HARLE-
QUIN *enters from the opposite direction.*]

HARLEQUIN

How now, good Toby? Art ready for thy walk, Toby? Ah,
there thou sitt'st as patient as a post. Truly, thou art the
doggedest dog in all dogdom. But what have we here?
Corpses? And Blood? Nay, 'tis purple, and thus we know,
Toby—even thou, a dog, and I, a Shakespearean clown, able
only to converse in prose, and not, like my betters, in
poetry—that 'tis royal blood. But ere we go I must, clown-
wise, commit a joke. Know'st thou, good Toby, why a
chrysalis is like a hot-buttered roll? Dost thou give up?
[*TOBY nods.*] Because 'tis the grub that makes the butter
fly! Will no one laugh? Nay, Toby, 'tis bitter work to play
the clown with jokes three hundred years old. Well, let us
bear away the bodies. Come, good Toby.

48

[*HARLEQUIN and* TOBY *exeunt, dragging the corpses.* KING
PUNCH *re-enters, horribly changed: his clothes are in dis-
array, his body bent, his face aged and marked with guilt.*]

KING PUNCH
Grim nights succeed dark days, grim days dark nights.
Sweet sleep, that darns the jerseys of the just,
Unravels Punch's garments and his reason—
Oh, god-like reason, sweater of the mind
That keeps it snug from madness' chilling blast—
His reason, like a drunkard, stumbles shrieking
Adown the murky tunnels of the soul.
Oh Metaphor, how god-like are thy uses;
Yet, god-like Metaphor, e'en thou art mixed,
Bamboozled by the ruin that is Punch!
Punch, who has bartered reason for a bauble!
Punch, once a king, now bond-slave to remorse!
Oh yesterday, return. Let Punch undo
The act that makes all morrows mockeries!

[*Enter* GHOST OF QUEEN JUDY, *dressed all in white, with
white make-up.*]

QUEEN JUDY'S GHOST
I am the ghost of she that was thy Queen.

KING PUNCH
Hence, apparition! Oh, mine eyeballs, burst!

[*Enter* GHOST OF PAULINA.]

PAULINA'S GHOST
I am the ghost of her who was thy love.

49

PUNCH

Avaunt! Begone! Dissolve! I lov'd thee not!

PAULINA'S GHOST

Nay, that thou didst: I have thy letters saved!

[*Enter* GHOST OF PRINCE OMLET.]

OMLET'S GHOST

I am the ghost of Omlet, infant prince.
I want my rattle! Father, give it me!

KING PUNCH

Oh horrible! A ghost in diapers
That seems to drool my soul's damnation!

QUEEN JUDY'S GHOST

Repent, false husband, slayer of thy babe!

PAULINA'S GHOST

Repent, false lover, murderer of thy wife!

OMLET'S GHOST

Repent, cruel father, killer of my nurse!

KING PUNCH

Repent? I do! I wish all acts undone
That bring me in such fearful company!

QUEEN JUDY'S GHOST

Alas, too late!

KING PUNCH

Too late?

PAULINA'S GHOST
Too late, alas!

OMLET'S GHOST
Yea, let Prince Omlet echo it: Too late!

THE THREE GHOSTS
Too late, too late, too late, too late, too late!

KING PUNCH
Horrible visions, trouble me no more!
Again I'll marry and a father be,
Again I'll love the nurse, and nurse love me.
False, whimpering ghosts, ye threaten here in vain.
Conscience avaunt! Punch is himself again.
I'll be no victim of a phantom's whim,
Let even Old Nick come, and I'll settle him!

[*SECOND DEVIL appears.*]

SECOND DEVIL
Who speaks my name? 'Tis Punch! Hither to me,
My boon companion!

KING PUNCH
Nay, it shall not be!

Stand off!

SECOND DEVIL
Nay, I'll stand near: thou shalt be mine!

KING PUNCH
Not if I know it, Devil. I draw the line
At ghosts and fiends and all their gloomy crew;

You'll only take me if I can't take you!
Come on, Old Nick! Know thou that Punch is tough!

SECOND DEVIL
Then damn'd be he that first cries 'Hold! Enough!'

[*A furious battle ensues. The excitement is heightened by
an accompaniment of fight music and trumpet calls from
the orchestra. When* KING PUNCH *seems to have beaten the*
SECOND DEVIL, *the* GHOSTS *intervene so that he strikes
futilely at them. With his attention thus distracted, the*
SECOND DEVIL *collars him.*]

KING PUNCH
How now? Punch ta'en? O triple-wretched fate!
First I a wife kill'd, then my Pretty Poll,
Then Omlet, infant in whose baby breast
My kingdom's hopes were mixed. And all for—what?
A rattle! O Punch, wert thou mad? Ay, mad!
[*He goes mad.*]
Methinks I am a child again. [To SECOND DEVIL] Good
uncle, give me thy hand. [*He takes* SECOND DEVIL's *tail.*]
How cold it is! Nay, do not weep, for if the Devil weep,
Little Punch is lost indeed.—Sweet Ghosts, how trans-
parent thou art! I shall cut thee into window-curtains,
good ghosts, fair ghosts, and hang thee in a little cottage
where I shall live pure and innocent until I die, a holy
hermit, loved and respected by all. I die; farewell.
        And as I lived the terror of the age,
        'Tis fitting I expire at centre stage.

SECOND DEVIL
Cut is the branch that might have grown full straight,
And Punch will never see St Peter's gate.

52

Be warned by the unhappy traitor's fall;
His fate should be a lesson to us all.

[*The orchestra plays the* Dead March *and guns are fired offstage.* SECOND DEVIL *and the* GHOSTS *follow as* KING PUNCH *is carried off. The* SPECTATORS *applaud, but the real* PUNCH *is discontented.*]

PUNCH

It won't do.

PROFESSOR

What do you mean, it won't do?

PUNCH

All that Shakespearean business. Not that there wasn't some quite good stuff in it, mind you. I liked that bit about going mad. Gives an actor something to get his teeth into. But the ending—

PROFESSOR

It is the only possible ending for a tragedy.

PUNCH

But the Devil beats Punch. The whole point of Punch's Show is that nobody beats Punch.

PROFESSOR

[*Turning away*] Oh, very well. If that's the way you feel about it . . .

PUNCH

Now don't go away mad. But you see how it is. My public would never stand for it—

Your public! Now look here, Mr Punch—

I'm looking.

You'd better get it into your head that you no longer have
a public.

What, no public? Me?

You're through, man. Endsville.

You've nothing to complain of. You had a considerable
popularity in the naive era when the theatre was simply
a vehicle for thoughtless entertainment. But you realize
that today things are very different. The theatre has
become thoughtful, and what have you to do with
thought?

Too bad, but there it is. Nothing so sad as an actor who has
outlived his time.

Outlived my. . . . Oh, no! There must be a place for me.
What about children? Children love me.

Sorry, old man. I don't suppose one child in a thousand
nowadays has ever heard of you.

54

PUNCH

Can this really be the end? Punch an old doll, worn out and thrown on the rubbish heap?

[*Enter a devil—not one of the Devils from the two plays but a very superior devil,* MEPHISTOPHELES *in fact, fit to appear in opera. He carries a wand.*]

MEPHISTOPHELES

Now, now, Mr Punch, I hope I don't see my old friend in low spirits?

PUNCH

And who might you be?

MEPHISTOPHELES

Oh, come, you know me. And I know you. I'll tell you something, Mr Punch: humanity can't spare you. If we let you go, it will be no time at all before the whole human race is living on government pensions and Canada Council grants. You don't know yourself. You don't appreciate your own worth.

PUNCH

I don't?

MEPHISTOPHELES

Not properly. You are the Spirit of Unregenerate Man.

PUNCH

I am?

MEPHISTOPHELES

You are the Old Adam; and without you, the human race would cease to be human.

PUNCH

You're very encouraging to an old out-of-work actor.

MEPHISTOPHELES

Don't be down in the mouth. If they've kicked you out of
the theatre they'll have to ask you back, you know. Mean-
while I know of a dozen jobs where the spirit of Punch
flourishes, and you can have your pick.

PUNCH

You do?

MEPHISTOPHELES

I do. [*He waves his wand, and there is a flash of red fire.*]
Politics!

PUNCH

Me in politics?

MEPHISTOPHELES

It's full of Judys to be bullied, Tobys to be bribed and
coaxed to jump through hoops, doctors to be given doses
of their own medicines, officers to be swindled, and hang-
men to be tricked. Are you game?

PUNCH

A whole new world for Punch!

MEPHISTOPHELES

A whole new world for Punch! The world is yours!

[*There is a loud cheer from the* SPECTATORS.]

PUNCH [*Sings:*]
The world, the world is Punch's Show,
They all want Punchinello.
The sky's the limit; here I go,
For I'm a popular fellow!

I'll make 'em laugh,
I'll make 'em cry,
I'll make 'em scream and yell—O!
Mr Punch
And Mr Joe,
Mr Nell
And Mr Lo—
Mr Punchinello!

JUDY, POLLY, KETCH, HARLEQUIN, & OTHERS
The world wants Judy, Toby too,
Winsome Pretty Polly;
Hangman, Doctor, Soldier true,
Harlequin so jolly.

We'll make 'em laugh,
We'll make 'em cry,
We'll make 'em scream and yell—O!
Mr Punch
And Mr Joe,
Mr Nell
And Mr Lo—
Mr Punchinello!

SCHOOLBOYS
Everybody loves Mr Punch,
Let the trumpet bray, sir:

The world's an oyster, yours to munch,
We will show the way, sir.

You make us laugh,
You make us cry,
You make us scream and yell—O!
Mr Punch—
YES!
And Mr Joe—
OHO!
Mr Nell
And Mr Lo—
Mr PUNCHINELLO!

[*During the last verse the SPECTATORS raise PUNCH on their shoulders and carry him triumphantly off the stage and down an aisle of the theatre, while the CRITICS scribble furiously and the TELEVISION MAN & WOMAN follow the exit with a huge television camera which MEPHISTOPHELES helps them to use.*]